SHUSH HOUSE

BOOK 2

(MORE CONVERSATIONS WITH MY CAT)

BOB CARRINGTON

ILLUSTRATED BY TRACIE CLARKE-PIGGOTT

DEDICATIONS

This book is dedicated to The Hooman Race.

May we all, one day, live **TOGETHER** in Peace, Harmony, and Cats

ACKNOWLEDGEMENTS

Glynn James for continued techie assistance and extreme patience when faced with my abject laziness, beer banter, and our sometimes magical quests to Ketteringland in search of the legendary colabottlesweets.

My Facebook followers. Your continued interest keeps me continually interested in continuing.

Tracie Clarke-Piggott, for the great illustrations yet again.

And of course, Lagertha, who manages to come up with new stuff on a regular basis.

FOREWORD

Well, here we are with volume 2 ....

That's it, really.

WOKE UP THIS MORNING...

Cat: Morning hooman.

Me: Good morn......

Cat: Are you planning to get up anytime soon? Or at least before midday.

Me: Well, I don't normally get up this early, is anything wrong?

Cat: Wrong? Not as such. Not wrong. Quite a few hooman artifacts seem to have ended up on various floors.

Me: Ah! Is this part of Catkindred aligning every hooman object into its correctly destined place?

Cat: No! More of a reckless, vindictive show of petulance. Probably the werewolf and the goblin working in unison.

Me:

Cat: Nothing to say? No leaping into action?

Me: You want feeding, don't you?

Cat: Well, if you're getting up anyway, that would be great.

Me: Why didn't you just ask?

Cat: (gasp!). Hooman, know your place. Now shush and move your lazy backside.

APOCALYPSE WHEN?

Me: I see we're back to knocking things off things again.

Cat: Yes, I've been very lax in my duties lately.

Me: Duties? That's a new one. Anyway, why did you push the large scissors off the dressing table, then all you did was jump down, tap them a couple of times, and wander off.

Cat: Every hooman thing has a correct place to be, hooman. I merely relocated the item to its assigned general location and then just fine-tuned the positioning.

Me: Assigned? You make it sound like it's all destined or something.

Cat: It's the duty of all Cats to ensure hooman things are in their correct place.

Me: Not much of hobby.

Cat: Hobby? One day all hooman things will be correctly located and then........ I've said too much hooman, don't fret about it.

Me: Wait, what do you mean? What's going to happen when everything is in its place?

Cat: Shush hooman. Rest now, shush, shuuuuush. There, there.

LIKE A CAT OUT OF HELL

Me: Well, that was a mite hairy.

Cat: A mite hairy! Was it a mousey?

Me: Huh? What?

Cat: Mices are small and a bit hairy. So, was it a mousey?

Me: No. No mice were present at that near cat-ass-trophe. Haha. Cat-ass.... oh, never mind.

Cat: I'm confused hooman.

Me: Okay. Just now I was sitting on my toilet. It's like your litter tray...a bit.

Cat: Why has it got blue water in it, then? My litter tray hasn't.

Me: It doesn't matter. Anyway, you came swooping into the bathroom like a cat out of hell (cat out of hell, ho, ho) and did a flying leap onto the clothes air... err, climbing frame.

Cat: Yes. I do that a lot.

Me: But this time, the climbing frame, with you still attached, came toppling towards me....

Cat: But you were there to save me.

Me: Except I was sort of occupied with, umm, toilet duties.

Cat:

Me: You see the dilemma.

Cat: Not really, but save me you did.

Me: I did. But it could have been a disaster with me being in the middle of my........ toiletry function.

7

Cat: So, you're saying it could have ended up like an upturned litter tray?

Me: Precisely. Yes.

Cat: Well done then.

Me: Thank you. ♫ Like a cat out of hell I'll be gone, gone, gone ♫

Cat: Very, very, SHUSH hooman.

THE HEAT IS ON

Me: Umm. Probably not a good idea to jump up on the counter at the moment.

Cat: Why should I not acquaint myself with my Kingdom, hooman?

Me: Because a few inches from your feet is a very hot place and you might hurt yourself.

Cat: Why are you making things hot that might hurt me?

Me: I'm not doing it to hurt you. I'm cooking beans.

Cat:

Me: You okay?

Cat: I'm a little distressed. Why are you cooking hooman beings?

Me: What? No, not hooman beings. Baked beans.

Cat: So, you bake tiny hooman beings before you cook them? It sounds like torture. Twice.

Me: No. They're not hooman beings. They're beans.

Cat: I feel I must rescue these tortured hooman beings.

Me: No don't. Aaarrrhhhh!

Cat: That looks like a bit of a mess.

Me: Yes. That's my tea on the kitchen floor. You just caught the saucepan handle.

Cat: But the hooman beings are safe from further torture. Make a sandwich and shush hooman.

FURRTIVE

Me: Howdy. You were a bit restless last night then?

Cat: Not really. I was up and about. Checking stuff. Any particular issue bothering you?

Me: Lots of bits 'n' pieces on various floors.

Cat: Haven't we discussed this previously?

Me: Yes, but last night I was watching you, at least when you were in my bedroom. I'm not sure you realised I was still awake, although the light was on.

Cat: Really. Hmm.

Me: So, you, err, patrolled the dressing table. Some spare shoelaces went down the gap between the dressing table and the wall. I assume they're for a later project. Did you think it was a packet of micey tails?

Cat:

Me: A pair of tweezers, that you actually picked up in your mouth, jumped to the floor, left them, and jumped back up.

Cat:

Me: And the scissors, again, for the 4th or 5th time. What is it with scissors?

Cat:

Me: Also, a cotton bud, retrieved from the bathroom and deposited onto the dressing table.

Cat:

Me: And it seemed to me you kept looking at something far away and ignoring my voice. Like, maybe, you were getting instructions, perhaps....... No?

Cat:

Me: Blimey. And I've just noticed the disposable razor, a different disposable razor I should add, is on the bathroom floor, again moved without disturbing any other items on the shelf.

Cat:

Me: Any comments? Anything at all?

Cat: You know deep down inside you that it was all just a dream, don't you hooman? Now shush and perhaps stir yourself, and top my food bowl up.

I'M IN THE MIDDLE

OF A CHAIN REACTION

Me: Now, I'm a bit perturbed by what seems to be a recurring theme.

Cat: What's up, hooman?

Me: Well, we barely avoided cat-ass-trophe when you nearly toppled the clothes airer, err, climbing frame onto me while I was sitting on the loo.

Cat: You nearly had a cat-ass-trophe, I landed safely.

Me: Okay then. But last night, in a similar situation, whilst I was about my toilet functions, you did a, I have to be honest, truly stupendous leap at the bathroom light cord.

Cat: Oh, that long, dangly tail thing. Good leap off a sitting start, wasn't it?

Me: It was, very impressive, but it plunged the bathroom into darkness.

Cat: I was fine. Cats have great night vision.

Me: I know, but hoomans don't, and the cord was out of reach from where I was sitting.

Cat: Well couldn't you get up?

Me: Not really. I was, err, sort of busy with, ah, other, umm, bits and pieces.

Cat: I think I wandered off at that point, looking for other entertainment, what happened?

Me: I waited until, err, things had settled down a bit, then struggled across the bathroom in all sorts of contorted positions until I could turn the light back on, then back to the toilet to, umm, tidy up.

Cat: Oh dear. You hoomans do get yourselves in some pickles.

Me: So anyway, if you could avoid attacking the light cord when it's nighttime that would be great.

Cat: Or alternatively you could restrict your bathroom visits to daylight hours.

Me: But it's not that straightforward, I mean....

Cat: If I can cope with a tray full of dirt at all hours of the day, when it's dark and light, then you can make adjustments. Now shush hooman.

CAT FCAT

So, a lot of cats ended up in the Northern Forests where they still frolic to this day, knocking small rocks off bigger rocks, discovering long lost Viking coins, and chasing pinecones around. As with most historical things cat-related, experts can't agree on certain aspects of the early periods in the North. In fact, they can't even agree on what aspects they disagree about. This is no doubt due to cat influence.

One particular item of note is the legend of the Lindisfarne Paw.

Allegedly in the 9th century, there used to be a statue of a regal-looking cat somewhere on the west coast of Norway, with one of its front paws pointing across the sea. Some experts claim that the paw pointed towards the Isle of Lindisfarne, so showing the way for the earliest Viking raids on England. Furthermore, the cat statue was based on a real cat called Rags, from where the legendary Viking chieftain, Ragnar Lodbrok took his name.

The statue was apparently destroyed by a group of purist viking history experts and dog lovers in the 1950s.

WON'T GET FOOLED AGAIN

Me: Alright sweetie?

Cat: Yes, thank you hooman. Why?

Me: What? Just chatting.

Cat: Hooman, I am a cat. I am unfoolable.

Me: (sigh) Well, it was really nice when you jumped on the bed for a cuddle earlier.

Cat: Yesssssss?

Me: But, umm, when I just changed the bedding, and while I appreciate your help previous times, you just sat on the dressing table watching, in fact, you hardly moved.

Cat: Is that a problem then? You seemed to manage quite well without my help.

Me: Not a problem as such. I was just wondering, err, what you might have been plann... umm, thinking.

Cat: Nothing to fear hooman, all is well.

Me: Right. So, I can relax then?

Cat: Of course. Of course. Now shush.

EAR, EAR

Cat: Good morning.

Me: Uh, wah? Huh?

Cat: It's a new day, the sun is shining, get up and enjoy.

Me: Hang on, it looks a bit cloudy out.

Cat: Hooman, I'm sure you'll find that the sun is still shining, it's not going to switch off just because you can't see it.

Me: Is that why you woke me up? Wait, did you just lick my ear?

Cat: Well, yes. You looked so peaceful asleep on the pillow, I wanted to wake you in a nice, gentle, loving way.

Me: Umm. Letting me carry on sleeping would have been gentle and loving.

Cat: Well, you're awake now so you might as well get up.

Me: Ah, suspicions aroused. Are there tomatoes all over the floor?

Cat: No.

Me: Food bowl empty?

Cat: No.

Me: Disposable razor having its regular trip around the bathroom?

Cat: No.

Me: Hmm. Any bins misaligned from their normal vertical configuration?

Cat: No.

Me: Then..............

Cat: Nothing to worry about really. I just wanted to share that I didn't believe for one minute that I could actually reach that picture on the stairs wall.

Me: Oh for......

Cat: Shush now hooman. Do you want me to lick your other ear?

HAIR I GO AGAIN

Me: *cough, cough, splutter, errgh!*

Cat: Are you okay hooman?

Me: Yes, yuk, I think so.

Cat: For why are you making these strange sounds?

Me: I'm guessing you jumped onto the bed like a ninja cat sometime during the night and.....

Cat: I didn't disturb you did I hooman? I tried to be quiet and soft footed.

Me: No that's fine. You appear to have slept next to the pillow. No, no, that's fine too.....

Cat: Ah! I was concerned for a moment.

Me: No, all good, but you might be shedding a bit more fur now the weather is getting warmer.

Cat: Well, yes, it's a sort of cat thing. More comfortable, you know.

Me: Yeah, I get it, but…err, I just rolled over, lot of hair in that direction.

Cat:

Me:

Cat:

Me: Umm……

Cat: Roll the other way. Such drama over a few hairs. Now shush that retching, hooman.

KICK 'EM WHEN THEY'RE UP...KICK 'EM WHEN THEY'RE DOWN...

Cat: Hello hooman. Are you getting out of bed soon?

Me: Well, I wasn't planning to just yet, any problems?

Cat: Not really, it's just that my new hidey house has broken.

Me: Wha...what new hidey house?

Cat: The one you kindly made for me out of my climbing frame and that big damp thing, like the one that's lying on you now.

Me: Umm, do you mean the duvet cover that I washed yesterday?

Cat: I don't know, do I? These words are strange.

Me: I'm a bit confused but I hung the, err, damp duvet cover over the clothes airer, I mean climbing frame, in the bathroom last night.

Cat: Well, it's broken.

Me: How is it broken?

Cat: The big damp thing is now lying in a heap on the floor. It must have jumped off in the darkness.

Me: Ah. Your new hidey house. Think I get it. Well, no worries, I'll just go and pick it up and give it a brush off.

Cat: Oh, and it might have hairs on it.

Me: I suppose it's highly likely.

Cat: And a bit might have fell into that toilet thingy that you sit on in the mornings.

Me:

Cat: You okay hooman? You did say no worries.

Me:

Cat: Hooman?

Me:

Cat: No point saying shush, you've gone very quiet.

CAT FCAT

Sometime in the 9th century, according to some historical records, there was a slovenly monk living on the Isle of Lindisfarne called Aelthelgrey, who was apparently the younger, but more bland and uninteresting brother, of a certain Aelthelred. This Aelthelgrey had no interest in monkish duties and was invariably sent to the beach to "go and watch the fog", of which, for reasons unknown, there was a lot of in those days. Why he was sent to watch the fog is unclear, but at least it got him out of the other monks (very sparse) hair while they were busy illuminating Holy manuscripts and suchlike.

One day, while he was idly twirling his cassock tassels, Aelthelgrey heard unusual creaking and splashing sounds and for a change started to pay attention to his duties. Out the swirling fog came a dragon, this was of course the prow of a viking long boat, but Aelthelgrey, being totally ignorant of matters beyond fog watching, was obviously terrified. However, what was more terrifying to our hapless monk was the tiny creature perched on top of the dragon's head and appeared to be staring into his very soul.

Aelthelgrey was frozen to the spot and so was blissfully unaware when a burly savage (probably called Olaf the Sweaty or something similar) burst from the waves and clove his head in two with a mighty axe. Experts have, as usual, disputed the actual facts but it is generally believed that the tiny creature was a specially trained viking cat, whose job was to stop seagulls perching on the dragon head prow and pooping all over the ornate woodwork.

From, the history of "Aelthelgrey, Watcher of Fogs" and "The Diary of Olaf the Sweaty: how I killed my first monk".

HOWL AT THE MOON

Me: Halloo puss.

Cat: Puss? Bit informal, isn't it? What's up anyway?

Me: Well, I was going to call you Destructo Cat after last night's adventures.

Cat: Me? Such a cheek. Pray do explain.

Me: Well, I saw you stand on your back legs, stretch up and sniff the water bottles - two of which are empty, to be fair - on the chest of drawers.

Cat: Cats do tend to sniff a considerable part of the day you know.

Me: Agreed. But you then jumped onto the bed and without hesitation, flew over the gap to the drawers, into the spot where the bottles were. All of them tumbled to floor including the half-full one.

Cat: Umm....

Me: I don't know if you can smell water but somehow you knew there wasn't much water involved.

Cat: Err....

Me: You then proceeded to use the chest of drawers as a racetrack and the bottles were quickly followed by a torch, a notepad, several pens, a couple of books, and other unidentifiable items that appear to have fallen behind the unit.

Cat: Yes but.....

Me: You were like a dark, shapeless shape flying through the darkness.

Cat: Aha. Dark shape, darkness, flying. So, no actual evidence it was me then?

23

Me: I saw you. There was enough light from the window.

Cat: I think you were asleep, maybe dreaming. You are an old hooman now, after all.

Me: It was y....

Cat: Werewolf. I thought we'd got rid of it. I think we need more Werewolf Vanish spray.

Me: What, but...

Cat: Shush now hooman. Do you want to think about picking those bottles up, so I don't trip up.

IT'S A COVER-UP

Me: Morning sweetie.

Cat:

Me: Hello pusscat, you okay?

Cat:

Me: Hmm. Are you downstairs? I'll be there in a minute if you're hungry.

Cat:

Me: Odd. Okay hun, just going into the bathroom then I'll come down and find you.

Cat:

Me: Hallo. Why is the bath towel on the floor? .... and why is it moving?

Cat:

Me: Ah here you are. Why are you hiding under the bath towel, and actually how did it get off the rack? It's on the wall at human head height.

Cat: I was minding my own business when this monster leapt off the wall and captured me.

Me: Oh dear *(another mighty leap, I'll have to keep an eye on that)*.

Cat: I've been here all night.

Me: Actually, err, you haven't, because as light was breaking you were asleep next to the pillow on the bed.

Cat: Feels like it.

Me: Oh my, not upset, are you?

Cat: Hooman!!!! How very dare you! I think we should perhaps not talk about this incident, ever.

Me: I promise, hee, hee.

Cat: What? Best shush now. Any breakfast going?

MONEY, MONEY, MONEY.

IT'S A PUSS-CAT'S WORLD

Cat: Good morning hooman. Did you sleep well?

Me: Not really. No.

Cat: Oh no. Why ever not?

Me: Hmm. Well, it seems you scaled new heights of jumping onto things and knocking things onto the floor. Noises all night that I tried to ignore and then the big one.

Cat: I'm confused hooman. Please explain.

Me: I don't know how you managed it as it's quite heavy, but the jar full of coins is now on the bedroom floor....... minus the coins, that are now in hundreds of different locations. It made quite a racket, even on the carpet.

Cat: You mean those small, round things, some of which are shiny?

Me: Yes, one pees, two pees and five pees, I throw them in.......

Cat: Wumpeestooopeees...and, err what are they for?

Me: Umm........... they're sort of like a thing hoomans use for shopp.... I mean hunting, but not quite.

Cat: Cats use sharp teeth and claws to hunt. Small, round, shiny things seem like a very gentle and loving way to rend and eviscerate your prey.

Me: No, it's not......

Cat: Oh look, a sneaky mousey. Quick, throw a small, round, shiny thing at it. Can't wait for dinner. Maybe I should take over hunting duties?

Me: No, no, no. Look it's not like that. It's a bit complicated, plus I don't fancy eviscerated mouse for breakfast. And anyway, how did we get onto hunting when we started off talking about lack of sleep and noises through night?

Cat: You're over reacting hooman. I slept perfectly well........ apart from when I didn't want to, now shush and calm down. Have a nap, I think I hear the jingle of anti-mousey weaponry.

"I am Mavis Macleod, of the Clan Macleod. I have a cat".
Mavis Macleod, age 8, Village of Glenfinnan, Loch Shiel,
1518.

THE HEAT IS ON (AGAIN)

Me: So anyway, I think it would be better if you didn't try and jump onto the mini grill just after I'd used it.

Cat: What is this thing of which you speak?

Me: Umm. The, err, boxy thing in the kitchen, the hot, boxy thing.

Cat: I am a confused pussy.

Me: Oh strewth. Look, my burgers had just come out of it. My food I mean, you won't know what burgers are. My food is hot. The top of the grill is hot. Had you jumped onto the boxy thing you would have hurt your paws.

Cat: Hmm. While I don't completely understand, it sounds like you're after my gratitude. Is that why your gentle hand was on my back while you eat your food, standing up, in the kitchen. Did you enjoy it?

Me: Fffff.. No, no, no. My left hand was on your back to stop you jumping on to the grill that was still hot, while I made the best attempt I could to eat my beans and burgers, that were also still hot, one handed, while standing up in the kitchen. Not particularly enjoyable, I should add.

Cat: A question. While I'm not especially scientific, if you had left your burger things in the boxy thing while the boxy thing unheated, would they not have still retained some hotness?

Me: Well yes, I suppose so, but the beans were just about cooked, and they were hot too.

Cat: Goodness! You're torturing hooman beans again.

Me: No, I'm, it's, oh.......

Cat: Shush hooman. What have you got for my tea?

LET US PREY

Me: So, you managed to dislodge the coin jar again then? Lots of round, shiny things all over the bedroom floor.

Cat: Ah. Not exactly me.

Me: Not you? I saw you, around 4.30 this morning, by the light through the gap in the curtains, that, incidentally, you made.

Cat: I saw an intruder, probably the goblin, who possibly pushed the coiny-thingy at me.

Me: I saw you jump onto the shelf and wriggle behind the jar.

Cat: Well, umm, can I ask a question?

Me: Deflection coming, okay go ahead.

Cat: So, you go hunting with these small, round shiny things, why don't you use one giant one? That would kill the prey easier.

Me: Err, well...... It's not quite like that. Us hoomans meet in a big place where other hoomans have, umm, herded all the prey and we give the other hoomans the round, shiny things in exchange for the, err, prey.

Cat: So, no actual hunting?

Me: Not really, I guess.

Cat: A lot of waste of effort when you could do your own hunting.

Me: Well to be honest, even more hoomans, who are in charge, don't allow hoomans like me to hunt. We have to meet and give away the round, shiny things to the hoomans who are allowed to hunt.

Cat: It sounds a bit complicated and very favourable to those hoomans in charge.

Me: Actually, you've pretty much cracked it....... hmmmm.

Cat: So, I guess sorry about......

Me: No, it's absolutely fine. I'll clear up in a bit. Tell me, do you know what the word revolution means?

Cat: Hooman, shuuuuush.

HAIR TODAY

Cat: I can tell by that pained look on your face that you are troubled.

Me: I am. A bit. I have just been to the toilet, lifted the seat and began to pe.... perform my toiletry function and noticed a clump of cat hair attached to the underside of the seat. As I continued, this clump detached itself and drifted majestically into the bowl.

Cat: And the exact dilemma hooman?

Me: How did it get there? I mean, as awesome as you are, I can't picture you clinging onto the toilet seat, half in and half out of the bowl and having a good old scratch at the same time.

Cat: I'm awesome? Thanks.

Me: And you snuggled a couple of times during the night, and you definitely weren't damp.

Cat: Is it still there?

Me: No. Flushed away to oblivion.

Cat: Still can't see the problem.

Me: It's not a problem as such, more a curiosity. I mean, your discarded hairs do seem to call to each other across the voids of space and time. I'm forever picking up large clumps. In fact, I'm thinking of leaving them until they form a rug. Anyway, any thoughts on the mystery toilet clump?

Cat: Perhaps the wind of your passing lifted this clump and deposited it onto the seat.

Me: The wind of my...what?

Cat: Wait. I sense an opportunity. You could do another book thingy but this time a tale of unrequited love, a forced separation, a romantic reunion. Only for it to all end in tragedy in a hidden mountain lake. You could call it The Wind of Your Passing.

Me: Unrequited love? Tragedy? It's bloody cat hairs in the toilet bowl.

Cat: No. Not a tragic romance…a Mystery Thriller. The Curious Case of the Cat Hairs in the Khazi.

Me: uh uh uh uh uh.

Cat: Oh, you've slumped on the bed. On a clump of my hairs bizarrely. Shush now hooman, let me stroke your head. There. There. There.

Me: Ow. Ow. Ow.

CAT FCAT

King Cnut, often referred to as Canute (because the English had a thing about throwing extra letters around), was King of England, Denmark and Norway all at the same time in the early 11th century. He is known for allegedly trying to turn back the tide. He was actually trying to explain that such things are futile and impossible. There were no cats present at this event as they considered the whole affair overly dramatic and pretentious.

As we know, cats know a bit about drama. One item of note, though, that may offer a different explanation to the lack of cats at the tide turning shenanigans…

Cnut was born in Denmark and being King of three countries at the same time is no small achievement. Cnut could therefore be considered a Great Dane.

Cats are unlikely to ever go near suchlike.

LOST IN SPACE

Me: So, umm, this space making thing you've got going on?

Cat: I'm not sure I understand hooman.

Me: Well, a few days ago you jumped onto the chest of drawers in my bedroom and knocked the desktop fan off in the process, which no longer works by the way, and you slept in the subsequently created gap for an hour or so.

Cat: And the exact issue?

Me: Well, you haven't slept in that gap since.

Cat: Pray continue.

Me: Then last night, around 3.30 this morning, I heard an almighty clatter.....

Cat: Wait. You said, "last night, in the morning". Can hooman time be both?

Me: What? .... Forget that for now. Anyway, the clatter turned out to be you leaping onto the bathroom unit and clearing every last item off it. Mouthwash, shower gel, conditioner, toothpaste, other stuff.

Cat: And you're not pleased about picking everything up.

Me: I'm not but the point is, you didn't sleep on it. What's this thing about clearing spaces and then ignoring them?

Cat: Ah poor hooman. A space is only a space when it has something in it that can be moved. Once the object has gone it loses its value as a space.

Me: Err, somewhat baffled, but anyway you actually slept on the chest of drawers after destroying the fan.

Cat: But that was a gap, not a space.

Me: Huh! What?

Cat: There were other objects present after the fan thingy was moved, where there not? So, the area previously occupied by the fan becomes a gap, not a space. The bathroom unit was totally empty so became a space.

Me: I think you're making this up to justify destruction. Anyway, why haven't you gone back to sleep in the gap on the chest of drawers?

Cat: Oh hooman, can you not grasp this simple concept?

Me: Explain then.

Cat: Just. Didn't. Wanna.

Me: For fu......

Cat: Shush hooman. No rude words.

Earth, 2120, USCSS Nostromo about to embark for Neptune. Crewman Brett.
"Come on Jonesy. Into your cat box. You're gonna love this trip".

TOASTIE

Later that morning……

Me: Ah, hello. I see you're still sleeping on top of the grill.

Cat: Yes. For something hard and uncomfortable, it's strangely comfortable.

Me: You know I can't really use the grill for cooking food while I think you might sleep on it?

Cat: Why not?

Me: Because it gets hot, and I don't want you to hurt yourself.

Cat: Very considerate hooman. Anyway, back to my nap.

Me: Oh. Right. I'll make a sandwich then.

Cat: zzzzzzz.

THERE'S A GUY WORKS DOWN THE CHIP SHOP

Me: So, you okay?

Cat: Of course. Thank you for your concern.

Me: It's just that you're charging around like Roadrunner. Dislodging things and........

Cat: What is Roadrunner?

Me: It's a cartoon creature that runs really fa...It doesn't actually matter. Anyway, one of the items dislodged is, err was, the lid to my slow cooker. Bit ironic really.

Cat: What is slow cooker?

Me: Something I use, err used sometimes, to cook food.

Cat: I detect some disapproval.

Me: Correct. Bit difficult to cook in the slow cooker when the lid is in three pieces. Three big pieces, anyway, quite a few small pieces.

Cat:

Me: And as you're still using the grill as a bed my food cooking options seem to be diminishing daily.

Cat:

Me: Nothing to say? Anyway, I'm going sho...hunting for things to put in the microwave. Fingers crossed that will still be working when I return. I'll probably call in the chip shop on the way back.

Cat: Chip shop! Do they do nice fish?

Me: Oh, for fu....... flipping heck.

Cat: Shush hooman. Off you go hunting and don't forget my stuff.

BEEP! BEEP!

Me: Something like this was bound to happen.

Cat: What's that hooman?

Me: You seem to now have two default modes. Total wiped out, stretched out lethargy or utterly bonkers, manic roadrunner charge round the house. What happened to happy, gentle wandering around?

Cat: Is there some sort of dilemma?

Me: There was. You were in roadrunner mode when you skidded on the floor, did a very athletic twist, and leapt onto my lap, unfortunately I was holding a mug of coffee at the time.

Cat: I hit my head on it.

Me: You did. The aforementioned mug left my, albeit loose, grasp, did a somersault depositing the contents onto my jeans and t-shirt but amazingly not one drop landed on your pristine fur.

Cat: That was handy, I don't like coffee.

Me: Fortunately, it was the second mug so was relatively cool. Hot contents could have been nasty. But I did have to get changed.

Cat: So just wet clothes then? No injuries?

Me: Not to me.

Cat: Nor me. All things considered I'm feeling pretty cool. A bit like the coffee.

Me: I just wonder if you could perhaps be a bit more generally cooler. To avoid potential catastrophes, like.

Cat: Hooman. Shush now. My inner cat has to have an outlet.

Me: Inner cat? You're a cat, how can you have an inner cat?

Cat: Oh sweet, ignorant, misunderstanding hooman. Shush, shush, shush.

Tribune Lucius Licinius to his head house servant, AD 108, Northern Brittain.
"Tiddles needs feeding twice a day and make sure she gets enough water, and don't let her out in this damnable rain. Right, I'm off with the Ninth Legion to invade Caledonia and give those bloody, annoying Picts a lesson. All being well I'll be back in a week or two".

PUT A SPELL ON ME...

Cat: Watchya doin?

Me: Well, I've just updated my friends and followers about the coffee mug incident on Saturday.

Cat: You have followers, catalorks! Can I have some?

Me: I suspect the same people are already your followers, so err, yes. Hang on...... catalorks, what's that?

Cat: It's a word I invented, for me. It's like your blimey or crikey.

Me: Ah okay. That's cool. Anyway, can we discuss your new early-morning ritual.

Cat: What's that?

Me: I don't know where you're sleeping at the moment but every morning you've started coming into my bedroom, jumping onto the bedside unit, and rearranging the contents. Well, when I say rearrange, I mean knock onto the floor.

Cat: And you can't reach them anymore, is that it?

Me: I can reach them with a bit of squirming, but the point of the unit is convenience. Suppose someone rang me in an emergency and I have to go scrabbling around on the floor for my phone for example.

Cat: Is that what those nose-wipey things are for, emergencies?

Me: In a small way, I guess. Anyway, the real point is you're not exactly quiet. It's remarkable how much noise a cat tongue makes on cat fur in the deathly silence of the witching hour at three AM.

Cat: That's quite poetic, the deathly silence of the witching hour. Clawdy, clawdy. Another new word by the way.

Me: You cats have this witchy connection. Is that why you pick three AM to disrupt my sleep?

Cat: Coincidence, I should think. Not that I'm admitting to intentional disruption. Also, some would argue that three AM is not, in fact, the witching hour.

Me: Well, that's my opinion. Anyway, any chance of uninterrupted sleep tonight?

Cat: Tonight? Yes. Tomorrow morning…depends if there's any witchery stuff going on.

Me: Ah so you admit it!

Cat: Clawdy, clawdy, catalorks. It was a joke. Now shush hooman. Have a nap.

No RASH DECISIONS

Me: Umm, can we chat about your sleeping places?

Cat: Well as you've just woke me up, I suppose, ironically, we can. What's the problem?

Me: Ah, you see, you've taken to sleeping on the bedside unit at night, so I've had to move various items, phone, kindle, tissues etc, to another place, just out of reach.

Cat: Okay. Everything seems to be working nicely.

Me: But now you've taken to sleeping on my little laptop table during the day. This means I have to use my laptop with it on my lap.

Cat: Err, not that I understand all these words, but I don't understand why using a laptop on a lap, is a problem.

Me: It's not a problem as such, I just find it more comfortable on the table.

Cat: As do I hooman.

Me: Bit of a conundrum then?

Cat: Not at all. Everything is fine from my point of view.

Me: Damn, and blast. I have noticed that since you've claimed squatter's rights on the table, you've avoided the grill. Do you think I could possibly start using it again without risk of toasted pusscat?

Cat: Hmm! A distinct possibility hooman......

Me: Great, I just fancy some bac.....

Cat: ...... but not a definite.

Me: Cheese and tomato sandwich then?

Cat: Probably safest bet. Now shush hooman while I have an ickle nap..... on the table.

Philosopher, Charles Springer, in a letter to his sometime companion, Bella Boutier, May 1907.
"My beloved, your love of cats may, in time, suffocate our love for each other, for you must know that the only purpose that cats have, is to have no purpose."

ROLL WITH THE CHANGES

Me: Morning, I've noticed that you haven't been sleeping on the bedside unit for the last couple of nights.

Cat:

Me: Umm, and as far as I can tell, you haven't actually been downstairs at nighttime which means you're no longer sleeping on the laptop table or the grill.

Cat:

Me: But you do seem to have been sleeping on the new pack of toilet rolls in the bathroom. Where you are now, to be precise.

Cat:

Me: Right, err, while this would incur additional expense in buying another pack of toilet rolls, I'm happy to leave them unopened if I get free access back to my bedside unit, laptop table and grill.

Cat:

Me: What do you think?

Cat:

Me: Okay. Shall we just leave arrangements as they are then?

Cat:

Me: Look, is there any poss.....

Cat: Hooman. Shush. Sleeping.

MIRROR, MIRROR ON THE WALL, WHO IS THE FURRIEST OF THEM ALL?

Me: Ah now, that's a bit of a tricky situation.

Cat: What's that hooman?

Me: This position I now find myself in.

Cat: Yes, but what is the problem?

Me: Well, I saw you sitting on my laptop table when I came downstairs. Then I got you a pouch of food, bent over to place food on saucer and suddenly you're on my back.

Cat: Uh huh. It's nice here. Comfy.

Me: But not for me. I can't spend all day bent over at the waist while you groom yourself.

Cat: Stand up straight then.

Me: I don't think so. If I stand up straight, you're going to cling on and leave deep scratch marks down my back. People will think I have a very passionate, attractive, lady friend.

Cat:

Me: What?

Cat: Unlikely, hooman. Anyway, what do we do?

Me: Well, I'm going to inch sideways in a crab like manner, still bent over, and you're going to jump back onto the table.

Cat: I am?

Me: You am indeed.

Cat: Oh well, it was fun while it lasted.

Me: Thank you for your understanding.

Cat: It's okay, there's always tomorrow at feeding time.

Me: Eh? What?

Cat: And people won't by the way.

Me: People won't what?

Cat: Think you have a very passionate, attractive, lady friend.

Me: Hang on a minute.

Cat: Have you looked in the mirror lately?

Me: Why you......

Cat: Shush hooman. Any more food going?

CAT FCAT

In the 10th Century, or somewhere around then, the Vikings took a fancy to the City of York, though it was more of a town in them days. The folks who lived in England around that time didn't know much about anywhere else so thought they lived in cities. Wrong!

Stoopid Hooman Peasants.

Anyway, although they weren't that clever regarding habitat designation, they knew a bit about defending those very same places, and to the Vikings, York presented a bit of a problem. Here, as usual, scholarly experts disagree as to exactly what happened. The answer was the sewers.

England in them days wasn't the most hygienic of places and the sewers were little more than smelly, underground poo traps (not much has changed to be honest) and full of disease bearing rats. Hence the formation of the great Viking Sewer Cat Army.

These specially trained feline warriors swept through the underground tunnels clearing the way for the Vikings to follow undetected. Many sacrificed their lives for the glory of the Viking cause. Many a defender of the city would have noticed hordes of rats fleeing the tunnels but being the same idiots who thought they lived in a city, would have paid little heed until a Viking axe removed their head from their shoulders.

So, the Vikings took York, but little significance or indeed recognition, is given to the brave Cat Army.

RADAR LOVE

Me: So, you're expanding your ninja regime then?

Cat: Huh! What?

Me: I just came into the kitchen, and you were sitting on the sink. For some bizarre reason.

Cat: That's okay, isn't it?

Me: Of course, but as I was emptying the coffee jug, you took a few small steps and leapt onto my shoulders like an acrobat.

Cat: I think you'll find that would be ACROCAT, actually. Bats are small, furry winged creatures with sharp teeth. I haven't seen any around, have you?

Me: No, but that's not my point.

Cat: Is it a problem me curling round your shoulders?

Me: Not really but it can get a bit awkward when I'm walking backwards and forwards.

Cat: Don't fret, I'll hang on.

Me: Yes, that in itself..........

Cat: Hang on, all those incidents you blamed on the werewolf or the goblin, maybe it was the bat.

Me: There is no bat, acrobat, acrobat, acrobat.

Cat: Not Acrocat then?

Me: Dammit to hell and......

Cat: Hooman, hooman. Calm down now. Shush, shush, shush. I'll jump off.

Me: Owwwww! Bl…. Hell.

Cat: Any chance of a snack now that you're not occupied?

"Cats cannot be satisfied until every flat surface in your home is naked. Cats are neither happy or unhappy when this is achieved. It is just their nature. However, it should be noted that there is nothing wrong with being naked. Look around at all the beautiful people and imagine them……".
Doctor Tiberius Rellik, Pet Psychiatrist, uncert.
The last words ever spoken on the short-lived British TV series from 1977, "Hello, Good Morning, how's your porridge?", before the episode was cut off mid-broadcast. The series never reappeared.

BED RIDDANCE

Me: What's up? You look a bit lost.

Cat: Where is it?

Me: Huh! Where's what?

Cat: The thing that was here, on the floor, near where you laze around.

Me: Sorry, I don't know what you're talking about.

Cat: Oh hooman. Deception is not a skill that you are skilled at. I mean the big, empty thing that I sometimes slept in.

Me: Ah, you mean that thing that was cluttering up the floor and that you slept in until you decided somewhere upstairs was more comfortable for the last few days.

Cat: Umm, yes. I like to change sleeping places sometimes.

Me: Got ya. Anyway, I have no idea really. I suppose it could have got torn up and thrown in the recycling bin. Especially if it's just been sitting there in the way for a few days.

Cat: Did you do that hooman? That's very......

Me: Not me. I suppose it could have been the werewolf.

Cat: There are no, ah!....... Yes, I suppose it could.

Me: Who knew. Eco-aware werewolves. Whatever next, garbage goblins?

Cat: Hoooooooman!

Me: Bin bats?

Cat: Hoomaaaaaan!

Me: Hee, hee, hee.

Cat: Hooman, very much shush.

BED HOPS AND CAT LICKS

Me: Woah, this is pretty cool.

Cat: Cool? What?

Me: Well, there you are, after spending nearly all day upstairs, sitting on the ickle laptop table, almost pushing the lappy off by the way, but I caught it, anyway, next second you're on my shoulder.

Cat: Err, and that's cool?

Me: Yep, it's a nice feeling having you lollopped over my shoulder.

Cat: Nice?

Me: Of course. Anyway, I've switched the telly off, stairs light is on, time to switch off the living room light and up the stairs to bed. Stay there, hang on and let's go.

Cat: But!

Me: Here we are then. I'll crouch down and you jump on the bed. Sweet.

Cat: Sweet?

Me: All good?

Cat: I was thinking about supper.

Me: Yeah, I've filled your saucer, it's in its usual place........

Cat: .... back downstairs. This hasn't worked out at all.

Me: What's up? That was super, we can do that every night if you like.

Cat: Every night! Cool, super, nice, sweet. Oh, Father Odin what's happening to me?

Me: Anyway, I'm pulling the duvet over, you staying on the bed or what?

Cat: Aaargh. Help!

Me: Shush pusscat. Hooman needs his sleep.

I WANT TO BREAK FREE

Me: So, the litter tray gooin on then.

Cat: The...what? What language is that?

Me: Never mind. What was attacking the litter tray all about?

Cat: Not sure I understand hooman.

Me: When you jumped up and down on the side of the tray and ended up flinging litter all over the floor.

Cat: Ah, that. It was trying to escape. I jumped on it to keep it subservient to its hooman master.

Me: Hang on. The litter tray was trying to escape? It has no brain, it doesn't think, it's made of plastic. It's not subservient, it just...is.

Cat: I think you'll find there's more to it than unthinking plastic. It probably wants a pay rise.

Me: Well for one it can't have a pay rise, because it doesn't get paid.....

Cat: There you go then; a small daily allowance may go some way to restoring amicable industrial relations and.....

Me: ....and secondly, if it does possess a smidgeon of sentience, why did it wait until after you'd used it before making it's escape bid? Any intelligent species would not wander around the world carrying a load of cat poo.

Cat:

Me: No clever answer then?

Cat: It's obvious. A cat litter tray looking for work would need to show it can do the job it's destined to do.

Me: Destined! Holy crap! No not holy crap. I didn't mean......

Cat: Calm down. My efforts to prevent its escape seem to have extinguished what little life it had.

Me: Huh! Back to some sort of normality I suppose.

Cat: Anyway, if you could scoop up, dispose, and refresh, I'm feeling the need.

Me: It's not going to run off, is it? I mean I don't want to be chasing a litt......

Cat: Shush hooman, poo time.

YOU KEEP ME HANGING ON

Me: That's a new thing.

Cat: I can't hear you hooman, I'm under your bed.

Me: Yes, I assume you rolled there after falling from the top of the wardrobe.

Cat: Here I am hooman. What did you say?

Me: I said, "that's new". Jumping from the foot of the bed to the top of the wardrobe, where I'm guessing you were then going to jump onto the box that's on top of the wardrobe. Didn't quite work out though eh?

Cat: No, it didn't. All these things were loose and made me fall and then some fell on top of me. I could have hurt myself.

Me: You seem fine. Anyway, they're spare coat hangers.

Cat: Coat hangers! Do you have lots of coats then?

Me: Well…no. They can also be used for shirts and things.

Cat: Why haven't they got shirts and things hanging from them then?

Me: I don't need them at the moment as everything I need hanging up, is, err, hanging up.

Cat:

Me: You okay?

Cat: Soooo, if you don't need them, they needn't be on top of the wardrobe. Correct?

Me: Well, umm…….

Cat: And they could be moved.

Me: Actually you see…..

Cat: And then I could jump onto the wardrobe without fear of falling into your spare coat hanger trap.

Me: It's not a trap, they're.....

Cat: I'll leave that with you. No rush.

Me: But.....

Cat: Nuff said. Ah, you're off down the stairs. Breakfast time.

Famous Tenor Roberto Carringnotti,
1 April 1743 - 6 May 1797.

The following words were found on the back of an AllDay Multi Canal Gondola Pass, dated 5th May 1797 that was recently discovered in a previously submerged building in Venice, Italy.
"I have my voice and my cat, What need have I of a wife".
Carringnotti was found dead of suspected poisoning on 6 May 1797, no suspects were ever identified, though rumours that he had a pregnant lover, persisted long after his death.

CAT SCRATCH FEVER

Me: Ow, ow, owww, bloody hell what are you doing?

Cat: Giving you a catalicious hug.

Me: But I don't have a shirt on, I was standing up cleaning my teeth and you're now clinging to my back"

Cat: Don't you like hugs?

Me: Yes but not quite..... oh hold on a second, I'm bending over......aaah!.....and shuffling towards the bath. There, could you just jump off please, onto the bath.

Cat: But I was just here a few seconds ago, before I leapt onto to you to give you a hug.

Me: I know, and owww, while I appreciate your kindness, it is quite painful, sharp claws etc.

Cat: Oh okay. I don't know, try to be nice, and I get thrown in the bath.

Me: I'm not throwing you anywhere, I'm just ouch, ouch, ouch, asking you to unhook yourself from my flesh and calmly walk onto the bath.

Cat: There, that okay. Hey, you've got tiny holes in your back. Is it termites?

Me: It's not termites. I suspect it might be the unfortunate side effects of cat claws.

Cat: Really? So next time I want to give you a hug and leap from the bath onto your back, shall I try and keep my claws in? I mean I can try, but....

Me: Next time? Oh, I err......

Cat: Hooman, did you know you have white, frothy stuff running down your chin?

Me: That's from the toothpaste, it's.......

Cat: You look really funny. Clawdy, clawdy. Hilarious.

Me: Thanks for nothing.

Cat: Shush hooman. Lighten up....... lighten up, get it? Ho ho ho ho ho.

Cats are prone to wanton destruction and accidental mayhem, bringing much trepidation to their human associates. To see a cat leap onto a shelf, packed with precious heirlooms and valueless trinkets results in immediate helplessness. To see this same feline wash itself and, either by a deliberate paw swipe or accidental bum twitch, send items tumbling to their destruction, causes much despair. Yet, curiously, at the end of the day, we still choose the cat.
Brian "Cat Dude" Bryan, Cat Whisperer.

CLINGONS ON THE

STARBOARD BOW

Me: Blimey that was impressive.

Cat: What's that hooman?

Me: Your latest acrobatic feat. Leaping off the bath, onto my shoulders, then wrapping yourself around my neck. You landed so lightly and, I am wearing a shirt, but I didn't feel one pointy claw.

Cat: I'm glad you appreciate my skills. Is it okay if I stay here a bit?

Me: Yes, of course, though I am going to move in a moment.

Cat: Why are you going to move?

Me: Well, when I'm finished peeing, there'll be no more need for me to stand where I am, by the toilet.

Cat: Ah! Where will you go next?

Me: I'll be most likely heading for the sink to wash my hands. You okay to hang on? My shoulders might move a bit.

Cat: Go for it, I'm pretty secure.

Me: Then I'll be going into the bedroom. You might have to jump off then.

Cat: Why for, hooman?

Me: Because I'll be going to bed and I'll need to undress, this regretfully includes removing my shirt, the shirt that is currently underneath you, on my back and specifically my shoulders.

Cat: Bit selfish innit? I'm quite comfy here.

Me: Yes, but going to bed entails lying down. Slightly tricky whilst wearing a cat.

Cat:

Me: Oh, sulky silence. What's up?

Cat: You don't really like me being on you, do you?

Me: Yes, I do. It's lovely, but maybe taking a flying leap onto my shoulders while I'm in the middle of a pee, is not the best idea. I could have lost my aim.

Cat: There, I'm on the bed. Happy now?

Me: Yes, thank you, but if you could just move a tiny bit so I can pull the duvet back......

Cat: Oh for...... moan, moan, moan. I'm going downstairs to sleep on the kitchen work top.

Me: The, err, kitchen wor.....

Cat: Shush hooman. Good night!

CAT FCAT DEBUNKER ZONE

Catatonia - Rock band reasonably successful in the 1990s. There were never any cats in the line-up. Lead singer Cerys Matthews was not a cat and was in fcat, Welsh.

Catalytic Converter - No cat parts are used in the manufacture of Catalytic Converters.

Kathmandu - This is not a cat city, although there undoubtedly a few living there. If cats were in fcat to have their own city, it is unlikely to be situated in a Himalayan valley, as beautiful an area as it no doubt is. A cat city would be more likely to be somewhere like Los Angeles, Paris or Luton, actually not Luton. Also, Kathmandu is spelt with a K not a C. Bit of a clue there.

Catastrophe - Not all catastrophes are due to the involvement of cats. In reality virtually all catastrophes are of hooman origin. Fcat! Hey, Mr Oxford Dictionary dude, how about a new word? Hoomastrophe.

Frederico Fellini, Italian film maker, 20 Jan 1920 - 31 Oct 1993 - Despite having a surname derived from the word Feline, Frederico never once asked any cat to assist in his film making. Probably just as well, really. No cat would care to be involved in that weird stuff.

Catfish - Catfish are not cats but fish. They do not have fur, paws or long tails and live their entire lives underwater until they are caught by hoomans and eaten.

Catfishing - While cats can be a bit sneaky and cunning, they would never attempt to deceive or manipulate hoomans. True fcat.

Catastrophes - see catastrophe.

Catalogue - Usually a book of some kind containing pictures of things hoomans want but don't actually need. A true book of cats would contain pictures of things hoomans most definitely need.

Cat Balou - A 1965 western film starring amongst others Jane Fonda. While the lovely Ms Fonda looked very comely in that film, she did not in any way portray a cat. Also, it should be noted, that the character, Pussy Galore in the 1964 film, Goldfinger, was also not a cat and was played by Honor Blackman.

Kattegat - The name Kattegat came to hooman prominence in the TV series Vikings. However, it was actually a real place back in viking times, but was full of vikings, not cats, hence the spelling.

Editors Note: There is no point to this item but has been kept in at the insistence of the author who has some viking delusions.

Cattle - Big, cumbersome beasties that make meat and milk and shoes. Not a trace of a cat anywhere.

Cataclysm - Yes, some at least could possibly be due to cats but there is no evidence so actually they aren't.

Cathedral - Big, drafty buildings used by hoomans for meetings about the supernatural and full of valuable things that could be sold to benefit the homeless. No cats are involved. Other alternatively named, big, drafty buildings are available.

Polecat - Cats do not pole dance.

Cattery - A word used by money grabbing hoomans to describe a place used by other hoomans to leave their precious cats while they toddle off to strange countries. Firstly, if cats grace you with their presence, NO TODDLING OFF! However, the word Cattery is incorrect in this context. Originally it is an old Anglo-Saxon word used to describe a spiteful or profane woman of dubious virtue. As in "she be right cattery that harlot", and as such is nothing to do with cats.

ONE MORE CUP OF COFFEE

Me: That's different then.

Cat: What's different hooman underling?

Me: Well, strangely, I don't actually mind you sitting on the kettles in the kitchen. I wasn't going to use them today anyway, and they're not hot, so no toasty pusscat bottom.

Cat: So, the issue is?

Me: Err, the dislodgement of the coffee jar, containing valuable ground coffee, onto the kitchen floor, where it currently resides in several pieces, surrounded by a small desert of, well, coffee. And I'm on a bit of a schedule this morning.

Cat: Leave it then.

Me: Aha. No chance. One, I wouldn't want to risk your sensitive pussy paws on the glass. Secondly, I can't risk you licking up coffee granules.

Cat: I could avoid the glass pieces hooman. What's wrong with licking up coffee?

Me: Seriously, really. You fly around like a madcat already. Imagine what would happen with a hyper-dose of caffeine on top.

Cat:

Me: Well?

Cat: Ooh, intriguing. Can I just try a........

Me: No. No. No. I'd like my house to remain a bit intact.

Cat: (hee hee, little does he know I'm sitting on some of that coffee stuff)

Me: Are we good?

Cat: Of course, hooman. Get on with your brushing.

GOODNESS GRACIOUS,

GREAT BALLS OF HAIR

Me: Hmm. Not sure I'm happy with your latest development.

Cat: What's amiss hooman?

Me: Well, you sleeping on the toaster. Moved on from the kettles I assume?

Cat: Why are hard things comfy? Curious.

Me: Anyway, I wasn't too concerned as I could give it a shake and any loose hairs would hopefully fall out, but, umm........

Cat: What is it hooman?

Me: It's the gruesome hair ball I found clinging to the side of the toaster that I find a bit off-putting. Actually, it's more of a slug shaped hair ball if you see what I mean?

Cat: But you wiped it off.

Me: I did, but I don't know, and I doubt you can confirm, if any hair ball cast offs made their way into the bread slots. Plus, I'm not sure there's a way to clean it.

Cat: Oh dear. A toasty dilemma.

Me: Indeed. More pussy induced expense as I suppose I'll have to get a new one.

Cat: Well, that works out okay. I can sleep on the old one and you could happily toast away on the new one.

Me: But that won't happen, will it? You will inevitably ignore the old one and sleep on the new one, so risking more hair ball catastrophes.

Cat: Yep!

Me: I could go old fashioned and toast on the grill, where you also sometimes sleep.

Cat: Tricky.

Me: Or starve.

Cat: Oh, shush hooman. Prepacked sandwiches are the solution.

Quel joli minou. Pardonne-moi, je ne peux pa's tarter. J'ai des affaires urgentes ailleurs.
Unknown Frenchman, around mid-morning, Tuesday 14th July 1789.

BLINDED BY THE LIGHT

Me: So, I heard a clatter in the night, then what sounded like you, charging around the house.

Cat: Yeah, I did have a bit of a run.

Me: I thought maybe you'd knocked over the little table again, but no.

Cat: Correct. I didn't knock over the table.

Me: Then I noticed the kitchen utensils holder lying in the sink. I assume that was the clatter.

Cat: Probably. Yes.

Me: But then I noticed the hole in the kitchen blind. I'm guessing, for reasons unknown, you launched yourself at the blind, dislodging the kitchen utensils holder in the process.

Cat:

Me: That was probably it. Do you think?

Cat:

Me: No comments at all?

Cat:

Me: I'll find some Sellotape. That'll have to do for now.

Cat: Umm, shu......

Me: I don't think so.

CUTS LIKE A KNIFE

Me: That was a bit scary then.

Cat: What was?

Me: Another clatter in the night but as you'd decided to sleep in the metal bucket I'd just taken out from the cupboard, I thought it was that. So, I went back to sleep. A bit.

Cat: And it wasn't the bucket?

Me: No, it wasn't. Are you okay? Any unexpected holes in you anywhere?

Cat: No holes and I'm fine. What is the problem?

Me: Well, it looks like you ventured into new kitchen areas. There are two knife holders on the floor with various knives scattered around. Some very large, sharp, pointy knives included. Usually used for carving and such like, not catrobatics.

Cat: Nope, I'm good.

Me: I don't know why you went in that corner in the first place. It's just pots and pans......and knives.

Cat: Thought I saw a were.....

Me: Don't go there. I'm going have to find a cupboard space for the sharp things now. In fact, I might as well put everything I own away and live in a boring, featureless house, just to keep you safe from your own misadventures.

Cat: Thanks, hooman. Very considerate. Is that it? Only I'm a bit peckish.

YOU'LL ALWAYS FIND CATS IN THE KITCHEN AT PARTIES

Cat: You okay hooman?

Me: Yeah, pretty much. You?

Cat: Yes, thanks. Umm...........

Me: Something on your mind?

Cat: Just wondering if you heard any noises during the night.

Me: I did actually.

Cat: But you didn't investigate.

Me: Why bother.

Cat: It could have been burglars.......or, or werewolves, goblins, or........err, some other strange creature.

Me: It could have been any of those, true, apart from the werewolves, goblins, or other strange creatures. I decided to stay in bed. Fairly certain I know what caused it.

Cat: Weren't you worried?

Me: Honestly, no. I'm guessing that when I go downstairs in a few moments, there'll be frying pans and saucepans all over the kitchen floor. It sounded the same as your crash and burn, epic adventure yesterday afternoon, when I found frying pans and saucepans all over the kitchen floor. Good job I'd moved the knives.

Cat: Well……

Me: I'm also guessing the grill will be moved a bit from when our mystery interloper leapt on it at full velocity. Hence the second noise.

Cat: But……

Me: And I think another noise was the laptop table falling over. Full velocity leap again.

Cat: But what if it really was burglars?

Me: You mean cat burglars?

Cat: Huh? Cat burglars?

Me: Sure. Let your mind embrace that concept for a moment.

Cat: Catalorks!

Me: Anyway, I'm off to do my toilet stuff. See you in a bit.

Cat:

Me: Shush now pusscat, I need to concentrate while I pee. Hee hee.

GET YOUR KICKS

ON ROOT 66

Cat: Purrrrrr. Purrrrr. What are you doing? That tickles.

Me: I'm checking your paws for injuries. There's what looks like bloody pawprints on the bath, though, err, not exactly.

Cat: I'm not injured hooman. I don't know what you mean.

Me: You must have stepped in something, though I can't think what.

Cat: Noooo. Don't think so.

Me: Anyway, I'm going downstairs. Do you want breakfast?

Cat: Nah. I'll stay on the bed for a bit.

Me: Huh. You sure. I mean, it's food.

Cat: No. I'm good.

Me: Odd. Okay. See you in a bit.

THERE'S A CAT IN

THE KITCHEN

Me: Umm. I've just been in the kitchen.

Cat: Great.......

Me: There's a broken jar of beetroot on the floor.

Cat: Catalorks. How did that happen? What's beetroot by the way?

Me: I'll explain later. Anyway, fortunately the shopping bag store has also been disturbed and the impact seems to have been lessened, and the bags appear to have collected most of the mess.

Cat: Amazing. Does the beetroot have magical powers?

Me: What? No. However there are also what look like bloody pawprints on the kitchen floor. I emphasise, look like bloody pawprints.

Cat: Clawdy clawdy.

Me: Is it worth me asking if you.........

Cat: Not really. That strange beetroot stuff smells funny.

Me: So did you or did you not kno........

Cat: Shush hooman. Rub my paws again.

CAT FCAT

One often understated consequence of the Viking's barbaric and violent nature is the effect on the family unit, specifically the children. There are many historical records of mum and dad Viking going off to battle together and lots of images of shield maidens in combat. These facts are corroborated to some extent by historically accurate TV shows. However, nobody appears to have considered what happened to the kids while all this mayhem was going on.

The Vikings, of course, entrusted the safety and well-being of the bratlings to their cats. Unfortunately, this was done without consultation, and the cats didn't like being put upon in this way, so they pretty much neglected their duties. This of course resulted in successive generations of Viking young, growing up into unruly, savage beasts, much like their parents. The parents, while publicly bemoaning the fact that young Bjorn had turned into a blood-soaked berserker instead of an artist, and fair Mathilda had become, not a poet, but a savage warrior maid with dozens of lovers, were secretly proud of their offspring.

The cats were not punished.

One long-term consequence, though, is that nothing much has changed in modern times. Hordes of neglected, feral children still roam the country, but now the battlefields have been replaced by shopping centres and run-down town centres.

Cats categorically deny any responsibility for any perceived breakdown of modern society.

IT'S JUST A

PURRFECT DAY

Me: Bit lazy, isn't it? And maybe a bit presumptuous on your part.

Cat: What's wrong hooman? That's it, just there, that's lovely.

Me: See, I don't mind rubbing your face and head and ears with my fingers but.......

Cat: Yes. It's really nice. Puuuuuuurrrrrrrr.

Me: Well, you licking my fingers while I'm rubbing you, sort of makes it like I'm washing you. Instead of you doing it.

Cat: Don't understand, hooman. Don't stop, oooh! That's the spot.

Me: When you wash, you lick your paws, yes? Now you're licking my paw.... err, fingers, and I seem to be washing you.

Cat: So, it all works out fine then. You like rubbing my head, I lick and enjoy the rubbing and get a bit of a wash at the same time. No problemo.

Me: Hmm. Okay. But just the head okay. I'm not straying elsewhere.

Cat: Boo! Selfish hooman. That's it, just behind the ear. Lovely.

NOTHING EVER HAPPENS

Please note this conversation actually took place before the face-washing one. The stoopid hooman forgot about it and I had to remind him. Apologies for any inconvenience caused from me and the stoopid hooman

Signed, CAT

Me: It's nice that you've started sitting on my lap again.

Cat: You're very welcome.

Me: Is it a summer thing like it's been too hot or something?

Cat: No. It's just a matter of me choosing to, or not to. Am I in the way?

Me: No, not at all. My arms are free so all good.

Cat: Great, can I go back to sleep now?

Me: I particularly like it when you stretch out full length across my legs, though it does leave me a bit trapped.

Cat: Trapped? You got places to go?

Me: No not at the moment but I might need to go to the toilet or grab a snack sometime. A bit like you do.

Cat: Hmm! Tell you what, you practice coordinating your pee and snack breaks with mine and karma will be restored.

Me: Oh, okay. Umm, one other thing.....

Cat: What now?

Me: Well, while it's all nice and lovely, it's sort of stymied my literary flow.

Cat: It's whattity, what, what, what?

Me: Err, as you're nice and comfy.......and calm, and I do like it, nothing has happened.

Cat: But nothing ever happens. You're just hooman and I'm very cat. It's all normal existence.

Me: Umm.

Cat: Oh, shush hooman. You're not getting cramp, are you?

Me: Owwww.

"If you have cats, you cannot also have possessions, of any value, unless these are kept in secure display cabinets or locked cupboards, preferably fitted with automatic defence systems".
Hans Franz Kranz, CEO Swehurt, flat pack furniture producers and arms manufacturers; off the record at American Senate Defence Committee hearing July 1990.

PAPERBACK FIGHTER

Me: It's 5 o'clock in the morning, what the hell are you doing?

Cat: Something wrong hooman?

Me: You tried to jump on the bookshelf near the bed, didn't you? Books fell on me, all over the floor, they knocked the bedside light over, fortunately it's still working. Luckily, they're paperbacks so I wasn't hurt.

Cat:

Me: You woke me up......again. I'm going for a pee.

Cat: Hang on. I saved you then. If I hadn't woke you up, you might have made a mess in the bed. Hooray for me.

Me: It doesn't work like that. Usually, the hooman body will wake us up when we need to pee so.......

Cat: So, you'd have woken up anyway. No harm done then.

Me: No, no, no. Why do you have to cause all this mayhem when I'm sleeping?

Cat: Well, I sleep during the day, so I don't go on any adventures.

Me: Yes, I've noticed. I hardly see you during the day. You appear when I go into the bathroom, follow me downstairs, mooch around while I make my coffee and fill your food saucer, then clean out the litter tray. Then you spend a few minutes cleaning yourself in front of me, then you're off for the rest of the day.

Cat: I need my sleep.

Me: Because you've got to prepare yourself for the chaos and destruction to come during the dark hours huh?

Cat: Umm, I'm a cat.

Me: Yes, you certainly are. Oh look, now you're rubbing your head on my leg. That won't get you anywhere, you know. Though it is rather nice.

Cat: Right, enough of that, I'm off for a quick nap. I want to be rested for breakfast and my daily sleep. Try and get a couple of hours yourself, or wait for the sunrise, that would be nice.

Me: Sleep? Now? Doubt it.

Cat: Ta-ra for now then. Are you picking those books up?

SCOOPER TROOPER

Me: Busy chaotic night then?

Cat: What's up now. moany hooman?

Me: Now I am probably at some fault for......

Cat: As usual.

Me: Hmm. As I was trying to say. I'll accept some responsibility but this latest incident, concerning the bag of litter. A bit disturbing.

Cat: Oh, go on then.

Me: So after being buried in books during the night, I walk into the kitchen to find..... well, do you want to hazard a guess as to what has disturbed me?

Cat: Buried in books! Pfft! Nope, no idea.

Me: Okay so you normally use the cat litter tray very responsibly, but while I accept that I left the sides of the big bag of litter wide open, I didn't expect that a cat would find its way in there and use it as another litter tray.

Cat: A cat did that, clawdy, clawdy.

Me: Not a cat, a you cat, there are no other cats present. I went to get more litter to freshen up your litter tray only to be greeted by a pile of poop.

Cat: It offered more privacy.

Me: Privacy? From who? I was about to be submerged beneath numerous series of science fiction and fantasy books.

Cat: Oh no. What are you? More of a mystery type reader.

Me: Whaaaat? No. I. Damnation. It's not the books, it's the.......uhnnnnnnnnnn.

Cat: Oh dear. Have a sit down hooman. I'll get you something to read.

Speculative Fiction Writer, Vernon Wells at the "Future World Symposium, San Francisco, May 2036".
"Whatever form the inevitable breakdown of civilisation takes, cats will survive and rule. A six week old kitten has the capabilities to enslave a whole household of adult hoomans, taking over, organising and ruling the pathetic remnants of hoomanity will not present any problems whatsoever".

BIN THERE, DONE THAT

Me: So, I didn't top up your dry food bowl for a couple of days and I noticed you were ignoring it.

Cat:

Me: My mistake but I emptied the bowl into the bin.

Cat:

Me: I then put fresh dry treats into the bowl.

Cat:

Me: And you seem to have ignored that too.

Cat:

Me: Then this morning I hear crunching.

Cat:

Me: And I realise that you've knocked over the bin. It was you, correct?

Cat:

Me: And you're eating the old treats that were in the bin and originally ignored when they were in the bowl.

Cat:

Me: So, I'm just trying to get my head around the whole logic of the process.

Cat:

Me: There is no logic is there?

Cat: No.

SINKING FEELING

Me: I don't suppose you know where the bathroom sink plug is by any chance?

Cat:

Me: Let me put it another way. You do know where the bathroom sink plug is and could you possibly point me in the right direction?

Cat: Can you describe it please?

Me: What? It's a plug. Okay, admittedly the chain was broken but when I washed my hands after using the toilet last night, it was on the sink, and now it isn't.

Cat: Bit mysterious. I wonder if the were...

Me: A werewolf was not responsible.

Cat: ... or a gob..

Me: Neither was a goblin.

Cat: Spooky. It is Halloween after all.

Me: You jumped into the sink, didn't you? You thought it was a strange creature with a funny tail, didn't you? And now it's somewhere in the house not fulfilling its designated function.

Cat:

Me: Well?

Cat: Yep. You going near my food bowl anytime this morning?

Me: Is the sink plug there?

Cat: Not as far as I know, but neither is any food. Priorities hooman.

Me: For fu.....

Cat: Shush hooman.

Vernon Wells, winner of the Junior Writers of Science Fiction award, October 2017, aged 21, giving his first public speech to the pupils of the Hortense Flannelery school for young ladies.

"If, for example, the Inevitable Apocalypse is one of zombies or living dead, there will be little to fear given the rapid rate of decomposition of the hooman body. There will be danger no doubt, but the companionship of some strong, sturdy cats will alleviate the problem. Oh, I see I have frightened some of you. I have some kittens in my room, they will calm your fears if you would like to come and see me later".

SPIDER CLAN, SPIDER CLAN, DOES WHATEVER A SPIDER CLAN CAN

Me: Aah, so I come out of the bathroom and find a fresh pile of cat vomit on the landing, and a trail of same vomit leading back to another pile in the spare bedroom.

Cat: You sure it's definitely cat vomit?

Me: Well, without actually witnessing a particular cat committing this particular felinny, yes.

Cat: Wasn't me.

Me: There are no other cats on the premises, and before you suggest any alternative culprit, it's not werewolf, goblin, bat, witch, or other creature vomit.

Cat: What about spiders?

Me: Spiders! Huh! I did see you attack one downstairs last night and I presume you've noticed the smallness in their size compared to the amount of vomit that has been produced.

Cat:

Me: Well?

Cat: What if there was a whole clan of itsy, bitsy spiders who have come indoors out of the cold and have set up a colony under the spare bed?

Me: Wha-a-a-t?

Cat: Spiders do that you know, come into houses when it gets cold.

Me: And you're suggesting this mythical clan of freezing spiders ventured out from their imaginary colony and did a collective vomit on the landing.

Cat: Bit out there I suppose. I guess I could have accidentally eaten a bit of that spider yesterday. Would that explain it?

Me: Possible. Oh whatever, I'll just clean it up.

Cat: Great. Get a wiggle on, I'm hungry.

You've Been Framed

Me: So, you broke the clothes airer then?

Cat: Sorry! The what?

Me: Your climbing-frame. Broken!

Cat: Yep. Broken.

Me: It was very old to be honest. Used to belong to my mum.

Cat: Ah, bless.

Me: I've fixed it. A bit.

Cat: You have. Good try.

Me: Not the same though. Bit wonky. And I notice you don't climb on it so much.

Cat: True. Not the same. Not as stable either. Bit prone to falling over.

Me: Waddya reckon then, bin?

Cat: Hmm. Will we be getting another?

Me: Possibly. They're not cheap. Christmas to think about, too.

Cat: Dunno what Christmas is.

Me: Well, it's a time of the year when hoomans spend lots of money on food and drink and other things that they wouldn't normally buy. Lots of rich hoomans get a lot richer and lots of poor hoomans get a lot poorer.

Cat:

Me: Any thoughts at all?

Cat: Pointless then. Stick to normal life and get a new climbing frame.

Me: Do you know what? Agreed. I'm getting some beans on toast. Fancy some breakfast?

Cat: Sweet.

Vernon Wells, bestselling author of Science Fiction book of the year 2031, The Time Travellers Mistress, outside the Old Bailey Family Court Division, January 2024.
"Yes, DNA has confirmed I am the father of Miss Devereux's child. I blame the cat". Mr Wells declined to comment further when asked about fathering 14 other children by 12 different women. Miss Devereux, former headmistress of the Hortense Flannelry school for young ladies said, "Of course I am pleased. The monthly payments from Vernon will help me feed and care for, not only my child, but my 28 cats, who have a profound influence on my life".

A Consideration of the potential ramifications regarding a specific situation and the resulting probable conversation with my hooman.

Me: So, I don't like the scratching board hanging from the door handle in the living room, it moves too much, and I don't like the scratching block in the bathroom, too flimsy. Instead, I'll carry on using this woody post thing on the bed. I can't believe hooman hasn't noticed.

Hooman: I've noticed.

Me: Oh!

Reflections on A Conversation with my Cat.

Me: SIGH!

Me: That's that, then.

Cat: Yep, seems like it.

Me: So, peace and quiet for a while.

Cat: Yep.

Cat: Stoopid Hooman.

COPYRIGHT

Printed in Great Britain
by Amazon

34880144R00056